GORDON AND

Also by Leon Rosselson
from Hodder Children's Books

Gordon Goes for Glory

Gordon and the Giantkillers

Leon Rosselson
Illustrated by Michael Reid

Hodder
Children's
Books

Thanks to Mike Perry

Text copyright © 1996 Leon Rosselson
Illustrations copyright © 1996 Michael Reid

First published in Great Britain in 1996
by Hodder Children's Books

The right of Leon Rosselson to be identified as the Author of
the Work has been asserted by him in accordance with the
Copyright, Designs and Patents Act 1988.

10 9 8 7 6 5 4 3 2 1

A Catalogue record for this book is available from the British
Library

ISBN 0 340 64072 3

Typeset by Phoenix Typesetting, Ilkley, West Yorkshire

Printed and bound in Great Britain by
Cox & Wyman Ltd, Reading, Berks.

Hodder Children's Books
a division of Hodder Headline plc
338 Euston Road
London NW1 3BH

1

May – Joining the League

'You haven't got enough players for a team, have you?' Gordon's father said.

'Yes, we have,' Gordon replied. 'There's me and Dave and Patrick. Ahmet and Stuart still want to play. And Mike said he would if we needed him.'

'Don't you need eleven for the Junior District League?' Mr Roberts enquired with mild sarcasm.

'I haven't finished yet,' Gordon said. 'Twinkle-toes and Mark said they'd play for us because Bridge Street Rovers broke up. And Clyde. He had a fight with Blondie so he's not playing for the Marvels any more. There's Daniel. And Davinder. They're good. That's eleven. And Oliver and Craig in my class said they don't mind being reserves. They're not very good but we're going to need reserves in case someone gets injured.'

'What about me?' Gordon's brother, Billy, piped up. 'I'll play.'

Gordon looked at him disdainfully. 'This is the under-twelve's league,' he said. 'Not the under-ten's.'

'I am under twelve,' Billy protested.

'You're too young,' Gordon said. 'And too small.'

'You'll be sorry,' Billy promised. 'I bet I'd score hundreds of goals.'

Gordon grinned. 'I'll chance it,' he said.

His mother looked up from the homework books she was marking.'Why isn't Denise play-ing?' she asked.

Denise had been West Side Wanderers' striker when they played seven-a-side football.

'She's giving up football,' Gordon replied. 'She's going to play basketball. Anyway, they don't have girls playing in the Junior District League.'

'Shame,' his mother said. 'I protest.'

'You're going to play in goal again, I hope,' said his father.

''Course, I am,' Gordon replied. At one time, he'd wanted to give up playing in goal because he was being blamed for the Wanderers' heavy defeats. Since then, he'd grown in confidence. Now he couldn't imagine playing in any other position.

'And what about a pitch?' demanded Mr Roberts. 'Don't you need a home pitch to play on?'

'Greenfield Park,' Gordon said. 'They've got junior pitches there.'

'Won't that cost money?'

Gordon nodded.

'And a strip?'

'We'll need a proper strip,' Gordon agreed. 'Red shirts and white shorts. And red-and-white socks.'

'And that'll cost money, won't it?'

'Yes,' Gordon admitted.

'So where's all this money coming from?'

'We'll all pay a subscription,' Gordon said. 'I reckon thirty pounds a year should cover everything. We have to pay to join the league as well.'

'I see you've got it all worked out,' his father observed.

'Yes,' said Gordon. 'I've done a lot of work on it.'

'And they've all agreed to pay thirty pounds a year?'

'Not yet,' said Gordon. 'But they will.'

'You mean their parents will.'

'Pocket-money,' Gordon said. 'Cleaning cars. Odd jobs. It'll be worth it.'

'Hm.' Gordon's dad looked doubtful.

'Please, Dad. George's team is joining the league. So are the Marvels. And the Polecats. If we don't join there'll be nobody left for us to play.'

'You'll be in your new school next term. Are you going to have the time to play all this football?'

'It's Sunday mornings,' Gordon said. 'I never do anything Sunday mornings. And Saturdays for training.'

'It's a big commitment. Can't we decide later?'

'No,' Gordon said, starting to panic. 'If we don't apply this month, it'll be too late.'

His mother pushed aside the pile of homework books and looked at him. 'You really want to do this, Gordon, don't you?'

'More than anything,' he said. 'More than anything I've ever wanted.'

'Well, let's be sensible about it then,' she said. 'You'll need an adult to take care of things—'

'Stanley's going to be manager,' Gordon interrupted nervously. 'He was a lucky mascot for us last season.'

What Gordon didn't want was his father offering to coach them. He didn't think he could stand that. He knew boys whose fathers coached their teams and they were always getting shouted at and criticised.

'How about if I look after the administrative side of things?' his mother went on. 'Open a bank account for you, fill in the forms, write the letters, make sure you don't get lost, wipe away your tears when you get beaten – that sort of thing.'

Gordon grinned. 'Thanks, Mum,' he said. 'That'd be great.'

'I suppose,' his father said a little grumpily, 'you

won't mind if I offer the team some expert advice from time to time. I do know *something* about this game, you know.'

Gordon was silent as if deep in thought.

His father raised his eyebrows.

'I don't mind if you give us some advice,' Gordon said at last, 'as long as you don't shout at me and go on at me if I make a mistake.'

'As if I would.'

'You do,' Gordon's mum said. 'You know you do.'

'Well,' his dad admitted, 'maybe I do get rather involved sometimes. But I promise I won't shout at you or tell you off. Is that all right?'

'OK,' said Gordon.

'Can I be your coach as well?' Billy asked. 'I bet I could tell you what you're doing wrong.'

'The trouble with football,' Gordon said, 'is that everyone thinks they're experts.'

The following Saturday, West Side Wanderers crowded into Gordon's front room for a team meeting. Everyone was in high spirits. They were excited by the idea of playing proper football on proper pitches with proper goals and wearing their very own strip with numbers on just like Liverpool or Manchester United or Arsenal.

'Listen!' Gordon's mother called in her teacherly voice. The buzz of conversation died away. 'This is a meeting of West Side Wanderers to discuss joining the Junior District League. First of all, is that what you all want to do?'

There was a loud chorus of assent.

'That means,' Mrs Roberts went on, 'that you're all prepared to turn out on Sunday mornings and train on Saturdays. Is that right?'

Another chorus of assent.

'Good. I'm going to be your administrator which means I'll look after the money and fill in the registration forms and book the pitch and make sure everything runs smoothly. And I'll bring along the drinks for half-time refreshments and pat your heads when you do well. So if you have any problem at all, you can come to me. OK? Stanley will be manager like last season. He'll talk about tactics.'

'And chess, I suppose,' said Patrick, and everyone laughed.

Stanley's white pinched face turned pink. In the beginning, the rest of the team, apart from

Gordon, had mocked him mercilessly because he was small and weedy and couldn't see anything without his glasses. What's more, he played chess not football. But now, though they still teased him from time to time, they had to admit that his brainy advice had helped them to think more about the game which meant that they played better.

Gordon's mum put her hand comfortingly on Stanley's shoulder and then went on: 'You'll also have Mr Roberts to give you good advice from time to time. He could have played in goal for England so he should have some useful tips to give you.'

'Is that right, Mr Roberts?' Clyde asked, looking at him in admiration.

Gordon's dad shifted uncomfortably in his chair. 'Um, it's a family joke, Clyde,' he explained. 'Although—'

'Now there's the question of money,' Mrs Roberts cut in. 'An annual subscription of thirty pounds has been suggested to pay for the registration fee, the hire of the pitch, the West Side Wanderers' strip—'

'Red shirts and white shorts,' Gordon interjected.

'—and when we have to pay for a referee. Can you all manage that?'

No-one said anything.

'Well, is there anyone who can't?'

Stuart and Ahmet put their hands up.

'My mum said she hasn't got the money,' Stuart said, 'and she says I'm too young to do a paper-round. But I can pay out of my pocket-money every week.'

'Same with me,' Ahmet said. 'My dad thinks the league's a waste of money but I do get paid for helping out in the shop.'

'I'll lend you the money for now,' Gordon's mum said, 'and you can each pay me back every week. Is that all right?'

Ahmet and Stuart nodded.

'Now I think we ought to elect a captain,' Gordon's mum said.

'Gordon,' shouted a chorus of voices.

'Mark,' shouted Twinkletoes.

'It's Gordon's team,' Mark said, 'so he should be captain.'

'Gordon for captain, Mark for vice-captain,' Gordon's mum said. 'All in favour?'

Every hand shot up.

'Unanimous,' Mrs Roberts said. 'Do you want to say anything, Gordon?'

'Well,' Gordon said, 'I think we need an aim. I think we should aim to come first or second. If we do that, we'll get promoted to the first division.'

'No problem,' said Patrick.

'It's not going to be easy,' Dave said.

'There are some good teams in the second division,' Mark pointed out.

'Anyway,' Mrs Roberts added, 'the main thing is to enjoy yourselves and play in a sporting way. If you lose, it's not the end of the world.'

'That's what I think,' Mike agreed. 'It's only a game, anyway.'

14

Patrick looked at him and frowned. 'I'd rather win,' he said.

'Let's drink a toast in lemonade,' Gordon's mum said. 'Fill the glasses, Gordon.'

Everyone took a glass of lemonade and raised it high.

'To the success of West Side Wanderers,' Mrs Roberts said.

'To the success of West Side Wanderers,' they all yelled and gulped down the lemonade.

'I can't wait for the season to begin,' Patrick said.

'Me too,' Gordon said. 'I wonder who we'll be playing first.'

2

September – What a start!

Gordon hadn't expected it to be like this. Playing football was supposed to be fun but playing against the Polecats was never fun. They weren't called the Polecats now. They'd changed their name to Park Hill United but they played just as aggressively and, Gordon thought, just as unfairly as before. Darren Walters was still there at centre back, loudmouthed and bad-tempered, lunging into tackles and barging smaller players off the ball. His father was there, too, a big bull of a man who was the team coach. Gordon, dancing around in his goal area, could hear him running up and down the touch-line yelling non-stop instructions, criticism and abuse.

The Polecats' kick and rush football seemed to intimidate Gordon's team. They'd boot the ball forward and charge after it, putting the Wanderers' back four of Dave, Mike, Clyde and Daniel under constant pressure. Patrick and Davinder playing in midfield hardly had a touch of the ball, while the forward line of Twink, Ahmet, Mark and Stuart couldn't seem to get their passing game going. They were tackled, pushed and stampeded out of their stride.

By half-time, the Wanderers were two-nil down. Colin Wright scored the first. He barged Mike off the ball and lashed a shot into the corner of the goal which gave Gordon no chance. Darren Walters scored the second himself, a messy goal from a corner which he charged in with his body. Gordon thought it might have been hand ball but said nothing.

The half-time whistle was greeted with relief by Gordon's team. They'd have time to collect themselves and rethink their tactics.

'Never mind,' Gordon's mother said as she handed round bottles of water. 'You're doing your best.'

'Just our luck to play the Polecats first match,' complained Dave.

'They're Park Hill United now,' Mike pointed out.

'They're still the Polecats,' Stanley said. 'They're rebarbative.'

'They're what?' exclaimed Stuart.

'They play armpit football.'

'Speak English,' Patrick said.

'Their football stinks,' Stanley said.

'Why are we losing then?' Patrick asked.

'You're not playing your own game,' Stanley said. 'It's as if they're frightening you.'

'They're frightening me, all right,' Mike admitted. 'I keep getting kicked.'

'Me, too,' agreed Twink. 'Every time I get the ball, someone comes at me from behind.'

'That's because they're passing the ball straight

to you,' Stanley said, 'so you've got your back to the goal. They should be putting the ball into space for you to run on to.'

'Their defenders are leaving plenty of gaps at the back,' Gordon's father pointed out. 'You're not making use of that.'

'Get the ball out to Twink on the right wing,' Stanley advised. 'I'm sure he's got the beating of their left back.'

''Course I have,' said Twink. 'Just give me the ball.'

'We can still win,' Gordon encouraged them. 'We beat them last time, didn't we?'

'That's right,' Stanley said. 'You did it by keeping possession, passing the ball around—'

'It's easy to say that,' Patrick said.

'They seem bigger this time,' Ahmet said.

'Oh well,' Mike shrugged. 'It's only a game.'

'If you say that again—' Patrick began.

Gordon's mum smiled at Davinder who was looking particularly grim-faced. 'Cheer up, Davinder,' she said. 'It's not that bad.'

'It's not that,' he said. 'It's not the game.'

'What is it then?' she asked.

'It's that Darren Walters.'

20

'What about him?'

'He's saying things.'

'Things? What sort of things?'

'You know. Calling me names.'

'Names?'

'Swearing. Calling me monkey. Stuff like that. Worse than that. I don't want to talk about it.'

'He's doing that to me, too,' Mark said. 'I don't take any notice. He's just stupid.'

'I'm getting some of that from Colin Wright,' Clyde said. 'Doesn't worry me. I'm used to it.'

'I'm going to talk to the referee about this,' Gordon's mum said. 'It's disgraceful.'

'Oh, Mum!' pleaded Gordon. 'Don't do that.'

The thought of his mother complaining to the referee was too embarrassing.

'Why shouldn't I do that?' his mother asked.

'They'll think we're cry-babies. It's our first match. Everyone'll know about it. Mum! Please!'

His mother hesitated. The whistle blew for the second half.

'What do you think?' Mrs Roberts said to her husband.

'We could have a word with Darren's father,' he suggested.

21

They both turned to look at the bulky, red-faced man further along the touch-line who was already yelling instructions to his team.

'That's where Darren gets it from, probably,' Gordon's mum said. 'Did you notice that there are no black kids in their team?'

'Well,' said his dad, 'maybe we should let the boys sort it out themselves.'

The Wanderers played better at the start of the second half. They tried to pass their way out of trouble instead of kicking the ball anywhere. Patrick and Davinder in midfield were picking up more of the loose balls and managing to set their forward line moving into the attack. They had two shots at goal in quick succession. Mark's went just over the bar and Ahmet's was easily saved by their goalkeeper.

The Polecats, urged on by Darren and with his father still shouting from the touch-line, launched themselves into the attack again. The ball was crossed into the Wanderers' penalty area. Mike, seeing Colin Wright charging towards him, aimed a wild kick at it and sliced it behind for a corner.

Darren came up for the corner, obviously hoping he'd have the chance to bundle it into the net again but this time Gordon, leaping high, caught the ball as it came across.

'Well played, Gordon,' he heard his father call.

The Polecats rushed back. Gordon threw the ball out to Patrick who, before a Polecat could descend on him, flicked it across to Davinder. Davinder controlled it, pushed it forward, looked up to see Twinkletoes waving his arms wildly and curled it out to the right wing for him to run on to. The Polecats' left back held back, waiting to see which way Twink would go.

'Don't just stand there!' Darren's father's fog-horn voice was quite hoarse now. 'Get in there! Challenge him!'

Obediently, the defender rushed at Twink who evaded his tackle easily, went round him on the outside and raced towards the corner flag.

'Come on! Close him down!' yelled Darren's father.

As Darren and another defender charged towards him, Twink crossed the ball. It was a great cross, curling away from the goalkeeper. Mark, running in from the left, met it with his head at the far post. The goalie got his hand to the ball but could only push it into the roof of the net.

Goal!

Gordon leaped up triumphantly, yelling 'Ye-e-s!'

Cheers and applause came from the Wanderers' small contingent of supporters. Ahmet and Stuart rushed up to congratulate Mark. Twink stood on his head and waved his feet in the air.

'You should have saved it,' shouted Darren's father at the goalkeeper.

'You should have saved it,' shouted Darren at the goalkeeper.

The goalie scowled and booted the ball upfield viciously.

From the kick-off, the ball was passed back to Darren Walters. He prodded it forward and rushed after it but Davinder was too quick for him, flicking it off his toe and slotting it upfield to Stuart.

Gordon couldn't believe what happened next. Davinder was a quiet boy, never in trouble, never aggressive. So Gordon was amazed to see Darren brush against Davinder and Davinder turn and aim a punch at Darren which caught him full on the nose. Darren staggered backwards. The whistle rasped out. There was an indecipherable yell from Darren's father. Darren was about to retaliate but was held back by his team-mates.

'What do you think you're doing?' demanded the referee.

'He swore at me,' Davinder said. 'He's been on at me the whole game.'

'I never,' Darren declared. 'He just punched me for nothing.'

'Send him off, Ref,' Colin said.

The referee took a red card out of his pocket. 'Off!' he ordered, motioning towards the touch-line.

Davinder trudged off, head bowed, blinking back the tears. He'd been stupid, he knew. He should never have reacted but he'd lost his temper and there was nothing he could do about it now. He'd probably be banned for the rest of the season. Well, he didn't see why he had to put up with being abused.

'You can't do that,' Gordon's father said. 'However much you're provoked, you can't do that.'

'I know,' Davinder said, putting on his track suit. 'But I don't care. He deserved it.' His face was wet with tears.

Gordon's mum bent over the boy and held him to her. 'It's all right,' she comforted him. 'Don't let it get to you, Davinder.'

'I suppose I'll be banned now,' Davinder said.

'Don't worry. I'll speak to the referee afterwards,' Gordon's mum said.

'It was a good punch, Davinder,' Billy said, trying to cheer him up.

Davinder gave him a half-smile.

Stanley peered at him sadly through his large-rimmed spectacles. 'It's a pity,' he said. 'We were just starting to play well.'

The rest of the game was a nightmare for the Wanderers. They were down to ten men, which was bad enough. On top of that, they seemed to have lost heart, lost all desire to win. They just wanted the game to end. Gordon tried bringing on Craig, one of the substitutes, instead of Mike but it did no good. The Polecats dominated completely and scored three more goals.

There were no sporting handshakes or three cheers at the end of the game. Gordon felt sick at heart as he walked off. He could hear Darren's father applauding his team loudly. It had been a disaster, a complete disaster. What a start to the season!

'Five-one,' Darren jeered at him. 'You're rubbish.'

Gordon ignored him. 'Just wait,' he muttered to himself. 'Just wait till we play you again.'

'Sorry,' Davinder apologised as the team approached him.

'What happened?' demanded Patrick.

'Leave him alone,' Gordon's mum intervened. 'He's upset. I'm going to have a word with the referee.'

'Mum—' Gordon began.

'I'm sorry, Gordon,' his mother interrupted. 'It doesn't do just to let these things pass.'

'Oh well,' Gordon said as he watched his mother march away. 'I suppose it could be worse.'

'How?' asked Dave.

Gordon shrugged. 'We could all have broken our legs,' he said.

'We could have lost ten-nil,' Mike suggested brightly.

'At least,' Stanley said, trying to find some words of encouragement, 'it can only get better from now on.'

3

October – Crisis meeting

But it didn't. The Wanderers lost two of their next three games. First Allcroft Albion, with George Harker in brilliant form, beat them five-nil and then they lost a closer match with Barnside four-two. The other match with Forest Rangers, one of the weaker teams in the division, ended in a two-all draw, Mark scoring twice, both after mazy dribbles from Twink.

At least these matches had been played in a sporting spirit; there'd been no more unpleasantness. Allcroft Albion had beaten them fairly and squarely and afterwards, to Gordon's surprise, George's father, an ex-footballer who coached the Albion, had come up to him to shake his hand and wish him better luck in the other games. Nevertheless, after four games, West Side Wanderers were bottom of the eight teams in the second division. Their one point put them level with Kingsfield Town who had a better goal difference. Something had to be done.

'Sack the manager!' cried Patrick when the whole team were gathered one Saturday morning at Gordon's house for a crisis meeting.

'Why me?' came Stanley's aggrieved voice.

'The manager always gets the sack when the team's doing badly,' Patrick said.

'It's not Stanley's fault,' Gordon said. 'We're just not playing very well. It was that first match against the Polecats that did it. We lost confidence after that. The defence keeps giving the ball away.'

'What about that easy goal you let in against the Albion?' Dave countered huffily.

Gordon bristled. He felt he was always being blamed when their opponents scored. 'You just gave George too much space,' he accused.

'We haven't been scoring many goals either,' Patrick said.

'Twink never passes the ball,' Stuart complained. 'He keeps showing off how good he is at dribbling and then in the end he loses the ball.'

'I laid on both goals against Forest Rangers,' protested Twink, defending himself.

'That was a miracle,' was Stuart's sarcastic comment.

'It would've been if you'd've done it,' Twink retorted.

Gordon's mum clapped her hands loudly. 'Before you all come to blows,' she called, 'I've an announcement to make. You all know Davinder was banned for two games because of what happened in the first match. Well, I wrote to the league committee to complain about the behaviour of some of the Park Hill team. I've now had a reply and they say that the Polecats, as you still call them, have been warned that if there are any more

31

complaints about abuse of any sort, they'll be expelled from the league.'

'Good riddance!' shouted Ahmet.

'We'll crush them at home,' Patrick said.

'Now do you want to spend the rest of this meeting shouting at each other?' Gordon's mum went on. 'You're a team, don't forget. You're all responsible when things aren't going well. Blaming each other won't help.'

'The trouble is,' Mark said in his thoughtful way, 'we're not playing as a team. That's what I think.'

Stanley took off his spectacles and wiped them with a grey-looking handkerchief. 'Mark's right,' he said. 'You're not playing as a team. It's like Gordon said, the Polecats discombobulated you.'

'They what?' exclaimed Stuart.

'What's that mean?' asked Ahmet.

'He's swallowed the dictionary,' commented Clive.

'Speak English,' Patrick said.

Stanley ignored them. 'The defence aren't covering for each other,' he went on, 'and they're just kicking the ball anywhere instead of looking for someone to pass to. That's why they're giving the ball away. And the forwards aren't looking for space and making runs. They're just standing still and waiting for the ball. And Twink's a clever player but he does forget to pass sometimes.'

'Oh, all right,' Twink said. 'I'll try and remember to pass the ball next time. If you lot can keep up with me.'

'If you played chess,' Stanley said (the mention of chess was greeted with a loud groan), 'you'd know there are two ways of launching an attack. You can push your rooks' pawns up the board or you can break through in the centre.'

'What's he on about?' asked Clyde mystified.

'Don't worry about it,' Patrick said. 'You'll get used to it. Stanley thinks we'd be better footballers if we played chess.'

'Well, you would,' Stanley said. 'Stuart and Twink are our rooks' pawns.'

'No, we're not,' objected Stuart.

'I mean they're both good wingers,' Stanley went on, 'but they're not getting enough of the ball.'

'Right,' agreed Stuart. 'That's the first sensible thing you've said.'

Stanley was warming to his theme now. 'So

sometimes we attack down the wings and sometimes we make a break through the centre. All the teams we've played leave big gaps at the back when they're on the attack. Their attack breaks down, Patrick has the ball, he sends a quick through ball down the middle, Mark or Ahmet, or Davinder – he's quick – race after it and before they can recover – wham! A splendiferous goal.'

In his excitement, Stanley was standing up, waving his arms about and making shuffling movements with his feet. They watched him, amused. Dave and Patrick began an ironic hand-clap. Stanley sat down embarrassed and began cleaning his glasses again.

'I think Stanley's giving you good advice,' Mr Roberts said. 'I'd like to see defenders joining in the attacks. Davinder, Patrick, Daniel, Clyde – you should be ready to run upfield. In the great Dutch team of the seventies, you sometimes had the whole team attacking or the whole team defending. Total football, it was called.'

'Yes, Dad,' Gordon said wearily. 'We know football's gone downhill since your day.'

'So it has,' his father said.

'Well, I vote we stop talking and go over to the

park for a training session,' Gordon said. 'Practise Stanley's chess moves.'

His suggestion was greeted with enthusiasm. They were all keener on playing football than talking about it.

Mr Roberts shook his head sadly at the rush of boys escaping from the house.

'They won't listen, will they?' he said.

On their way to the park, Gordon, Dave and Patrick debated the possibility of the Wanderers being promoted at the end of the season. Gordon was still convinced it could be done.

'It's a bit late for that,' Dave argued. 'We're already eleven points behind the Albion.'

'Yeah, *and* we haven't played St George's yet,' Patrick said. 'They're supposed to be even better than the Albion.'

'What about Mill Lane Marvels?' Dave said. 'They've only lost one game so far.'

'At least,' Mike said, joining in the argument, 'we can't be relegated.'

'How come you're always so cheerful, Mike?' Patrick asked sarcastically.

'Well, it's true,' Mike said. 'Even if we come

bottom, we can't go down. There's nowhere to go down to.'

'We won't come bottom,' Gordon said. 'No way. And even if we don't get promoted, we could do well in the League Cup.'

'Fat chance,' Dave said. 'The first division teams are going to be in that.'

'Haven't you ever heard of giantkillers?' Gordon said. 'Little teams are always beating big teams in cup games.'

'You're dreaming,' Dave said.

'That's right,' said Gordon. 'Why not?'

They practised passing moves in the training session. They practised heading. They practised dribbling. They practised taking near post corners with Patrick, their tallest player, planted in a position to head the ball backwards. They practised taking corners long with Mark coming in at the far post to head the ball home. The trouble was that neither Twink nor Stuart, who took the corners, found it easy to direct the ball accurately.

After that, they played five-a-side games with no-one allowed to hold on to the ball so that they had to control and pass it at top speed. Finally, there was the usual penalty shoot-out. They'd

never yet been in a game where a penalty shoot-out was needed but Gordon said it was a good idea to be prepared just in case. Mark, Stuart, Patrick, Davinder and Daniel were the best penalty takers and Gordon saved five out of the thirteen penalties.

They were in good spirits as they left the park. It had been a useful practice. The next morning's match was against Kingswood Town, probably the weakest team in the league.

'Be here at ten fifteen,' Gordon called out to his team. 'We should beat Kingswood easily.'

'You'll never beat anyone. You're rubbish!' blared out a hostile voice from behind them.

Everyone turned round. Darren Walters and two boys Gordon didn't know were following them out of the park. Gordon was startled. How come he hadn't seen them before? Had they been watching the training session all the time?

Darren stared at Davinder, raised an arm and pointed. 'That's him,' he shouted. 'That's the one.'

Instinctively, Patrick, Gordon, Mark and Clyde formed a wall round Davinder as if to protect him. But Darren and the two boys made no move. They just stared balefully, Darren's accusing finger still pointing.

Davinder clenched his fists. He was trembling slightly. Gordon put his arm round his shoulder.

'Don't take any notice,' he said. 'They're not worth it.'

They moved off down the road in a close group, Gordon glancing back from time to time to see if they were being followed. They weren't. Soon Darren and his friends were out of sight.

'Better keep out of their way,' Gordon advised Davinder.

'Don't worry,' Davinder said. 'If I see them coming, you won't see me for dust.'

Gordon and Dave walked home together.

'It was a good practice,' Dave said.

'Yeah,' Gordon said. 'Pity Darren Walters had to spoil it.'

'Those Polecats,' Dave said. 'They spoil everything.'

'Sometimes,' Gordon mused, 'I wish we just played football for fun.'

4

November – The tide turns

Gordon wasn't as confident as he pretended about his team beating Kingswood. They started nervously and could have been a goal behind in the first five minutes. Dave, in attempting to head the ball clear, only succeeded in giving it to the

Kingswood left winger who found himself with a free run on goal. Gordon came out to narrow the angle but the shot along the ground evaded his grasp and was going into the corner. Fortunately, Daniel, running back, just managed to get a foot to it and turn it round the post for a corner. In doing so, he collided with the post and ended up in the back of the net.

'You all right?' Gordon asked anxiously, bending over him.

'I think so,' Daniel said, sitting up and holding his head.

Gordon's mum arrived with a bucket of water and a sponge. She sponged away a trickle of blood from his forehead.

'Perhaps you ought to come off,' she suggested. 'Put one of the substitutes on.'

'I'm all right, Mrs Roberts. Honest. It's nothing.'

'Well, if you're sure. But let me know if you have a headache or anything.'

'I'm fine,' Daniel said, getting to his feet.

'Brilliant bit of defending, Daniel,' Gordon said.

'And brave,' added his mum as she jogged back to the touch-line.

That, Gordon felt, was a turning point in the

game. Conceding a goal then would have been disastrous for their confidence. As it was, their escape led them to believe that it was going to be their day. This belief was borne out when they scored an easy goal ten minutes into the first half. The Kingswood goalkeeper fumbled a shot from Mark and Ahmet only had to tap the ball into the empty net.

The second goal, five minutes later, had Stanley jumping up and down on the touch-line with delight. Kingswood pushed up for a corner. Gordon caught the ball and drop-kicked it out. Davinder trapped it, turned and saw that the Kingswood players hadn't bothered to run back and that their defenders were all over the place. He looked at Mark standing just inside the Kingswood half and directed a pass straight down the middle between two defenders. Mark, alert to the pass, raced after it. The goalkeeper ran out but Mark chipped the ball over his head and into the net.

Some of the Kingswood team protested that Mark had been offside but the referee pointed out that when the pass had been made, there were two Kingswood defenders between Mark and the goal.

The third goal, just before half-time, came from Twink's corner. Everybody missed it and Mark, two yards from goal, volleyed it in.

Billy on the touch-line started to chant: 'Easy! Easy!' until his father told him to leave off.

The Wanderers were well on top in the second half. They were almost constantly on the attack but somehow couldn't make their superiority tell.

'We haven't got the killer instinct,' Gordon muttered to himself as he watched yet another Wanderers' attack end with the ball flying harmlessly over the bar.

Then, completely against the run of play, Kingswood scored. Slack defending allowed their striker time and space to shoot from just outside the penalty area. Gordon, who'd hardly had a save to make the whole game, dived to his left but the ball hit the inside of the post and rebounded into the net.

This seemed to put some urgency back into the Wanderers' attack. Straight from the restart, the ball went out to Stuart on the left wing. He beat his marker and crossed the ball. It went out to Twink who was coming in from the right. He nutmegged the left back, waltzed round the goalie and lashed the ball into the goal.

That was the end of the scoring. The Wanderers won four-one, which, at least, lifted them off the bottom of the table and improved their goal difference. They walked off the pitch to the applause of their supporters, a 'Well done!' from Gordon's mum and a 'Splendiferous' from Stanley.

'That's the best you've played all season,' Gordon's dad said.

'You should have scored more goals,' Billy said.

'He's right,' Gordon said, agreeing with his brother for once. 'We let them off lightly.'

'We won, didn't we?' said Stuart, feeling he was being criticised.

'I know but we eased up when we were ahead. That could be fatal against a better team.'

Stuart took a swig of water. 'Well, I reckon four-one's a good result,' he said.

'Yeah, OK,' admitted Gordon. 'I just hope we play as well as that in the League Cup.'

'Who're we playing?' asked Patrick.

'I don't know yet,' Gordon said.

'As long as it's not the Albion,' said Patrick.

'Or St George's,' said Dave.

'Or the Marvels,' said Mike.

'Or the Polecats,' said Davinder.

'Maybe it'll be Kingswood again,' Gordon said hopefully. 'It's about time we had some luck.'

It wasn't Kingswood but it was the next best thing. It was Forest Rangers, the team they'd already drawn with. Only the second division teams played in this round. With twelve teams in the first division and eight in the second, there had to be a preliminary round to reduce the number to sixteen.

It was a cold blustery day when the match against Forest Rangers was played. Gordon noticed during the warm-up that if he kicked the ball into the wind, the gusts were often so powerful, they caught the ball and hurled it back again.

'If you win the toss,' Stanley advised, 'kick with the wind first half.'

'Why?' asked Gordon.

'You could be five goals up by half-time if you play it right. They'll get discouraged.'

Makes sense, Gordon thought as the referee called the captains together.

Gordon called correctly.

'We're playing with the wind in the first half,' Stanley told the team. 'So high balls into the goal area. Shoot from any distance. The wind could blow it into the goal.'

'That's not like you, Stanley,' Dave remarked. 'I thought you wanted us to play beautiful football.'

'Well, yes,' Stanley said. 'Usually. But I just remembered the first rule of chess.'

'What's that?' asked Mike.

'Always place your opponent with the sun in his eyes,' Stanley said, grinning inanely.

'Sneaky,' Patrick said.

'What about the second half?' asked Davinder. 'We'll have the wind against us.'

'Play it on the ground,' Stanley said. 'Keep possession. No high balls.'

'He's right,' Gordon said.

'Clever clogs,' Patrick said, patting Stanley's head.

'They've got a lot of supporters,' Dave observed as they took up their positions. 'More than us.'

'I hope their coach doesn't yell instructions all the time like he did in the last game,' Gordon said.

'I bet he will. He's the goalie's father,' Dave pointed out.

'At least, my dad's stopped doing that,' Gordon said. 'It used to drive me mad.'

It wasn't a very skilful game of football. Both sides found that the wind made it almost impossible to control the ball or pass it accurately. Forest Rangers couldn't clear it from their own half and the Wanderers' centres and goal attempts were mostly blown off course.

A series of loud commands was being launched from the touch-line by the Rangers' coach: 'Get in there! . . . Keep it tight! . . . Worry him! Worry him! . . . Get a challenge in! . . . Pass the ball! . . . You're getting caught square!'

'I don't know why they bother,' Gordon muttered to himself.

Their goalkeeper, in particular, was a target for the coach's criticism: 'Don't stand there, Trevor! . . . Come out! . . . Narrow the angle! . . . Stand your ground! . . . Catch it, don't punch it! . . . You're out of position!'

And yet, Gordon thought sympathetically, Trevor, a tall, slim boy, was playing pretty well. He made three good saves from long shots and then one brilliant one from Twink's shot which he managed to tip over the bar. Twink's corner was wasted, the ball being blown harmlessly over the line for a goal-kick. The goalkeeper took it and, just at that moment, the wind seemed to gather strength. The ball only travelled as far as Mark, standing about ten yards from where the kick was taken. He trapped the ball, took it a few strides forward and let fly. It zoomed into the net with Trevor completely beaten.

Immediately, a volley of abuse exploded from the touch-line. 'You stupid idiot! What did you wanna do that for? Haven't you got any sense?' until even Gordon's ears were burning.

It's bad enough making a mistake, Gordon thought to himself, without being shouted at as well.

The second and third goals arrived soon afterwards. First, the goalie failed to cut out a low cross from Twink, and Stuart was at the far post to knock the ball in with his knee. Then, from the kick-off, a pass forward was intercepted by Patrick, who booted the ball upfield. Their central defender attempted to head the ball out but it bounced out to Twink on the right touch-line. He swung the ball into the Rangers' goal area. It was meant to be a pass to Mark running forward but the wind caught the ball and swirled it over the goalkeeper's despairing leap and into the goal.

Each goal produced an outburst from the coach. Gordon could see their goalie losing confidence. He was shrinking into himself. His shoulders were hunched, his head was dropping. Gordon felt for him. He wanted to go over and reassure him, tell him it wasn't his fault. The wind was making it impossible to judge the flight of the ball.

Just before half-time, the Wanderers scored a fourth goal. Again the wind played a part. Mark played a quick one-two with Ahmet which left him with a clear run on goal. The goalkeeper, who seemed confused by the instructions being yelled at him by his father, stayed on his line. He seemed to have Mark's shot well covered but, at the last minute, the wind swept the ball out of his reach and into the goal.

He put his hands on his hips and stared at the ground. The yells from the touch-line were being tossed about and distorted by the wind. Suddenly, Trevor took off his gloves, hurled them to the ground and ran off the pitch. He didn't stop running.

'Hey!' yelled his father, setting off after him. 'Where do you think you're going?'

Perplexed, the referee decided to blow the half-time whistle.

When the game was due to restart, Gordon glanced over to the Rangers' team. They were in a huddle and gave no sign that they wanted to resume play. Neither the goalie nor his father had returned. The Rangers' captain wandered disconsolately over to Gordon.

'We'll give you the game,' he said. 'We've lost our goalie and our coach. No-one wants to go in goal. We're four-nil down. It's not worth carrying on.'

'Sorry,' said Gordon.

They went to explain the situation to the referee.

'I've never heard of anything like that before,' he said. 'Giving up in the middle of a game!'

The Rangers' captain shrugged. 'What's the point?' he said as he walked away.

'Well, it looks as if you're in the last sixteen,' the referee told Gordon.

'I think we'd have won anyway,' Gordon said.

But it was a subdued rather than a triumphant Wanderers' team that made their way home.

Gordon phoned Dave a few days later. 'Guess who we're playing next in the League Cup,' he said.

'Tottenham Hotspur?' joked Dave. 'Manchester United? A team from Mars?'

'A team from hell, more like,' Gordon said. 'We're playing the Polecats again. The first Sunday in December. At home.'

5

December – The crunch game

Gordon and Dave were walking home from school, earnestly discussing the best way to beat the Polecats, when they were approached by a fair-haired boy.

'You're Gordon, aren't you?' he said.

'And you're a Polecat,' Dave said rudely.

The boy flushed. Gordon hadn't recognised him at first. Now he realised who he was – the left winger in the Park Hill United team.

'What do you want?' Gordon demanded.

'I don't play for Darren's team any more,' the boy said. 'I got fed up with him and his father. They're both big bullies. I hate them.'

'Well, you can't play for us,' Gordon said. 'You're not registered and anyway we've already got enough players.'

The boy shook his head. 'It's not that,' he said. 'I came to warn you.'

'What about?'

'I heard them talking,' the boy continued. 'Darren and Colin and a few others. That Indian boy in your team—'

'Davinder?'

'They're going to get him.'

'Get him? What do you mean?'

'They're going to do something bad to him during the game. Make it look like an accident. Something like that.'

'They can't,' Gordon said. 'The referee'll send them off.'

'They'll do it when the referee's not looking,' the boy said. 'I don't know. That's what I heard them say. Maybe they were just talking big. They're always doing that.'

'Well, thanks anyway,' Gordon said.

The boy shrugged. 'I hope you win,' he said and ran off.

'What do you think?' Gordon asked Dave.

'Maybe it'd be better if Davinder didn't play,' suggested Dave.

'It's sick,' Gordon said. 'It's supposed to be a game of football not a war.'

'With the Polecats, it's both,' Dave commented.

'If we don't play Davinder,' Gordon said, 'it'll be like we've given in to them.'

'Yeah, but supposing he did play and they crippled him or something?'

Gordon sighed. 'What a decision,' he said.

'You're the captain,' Dave said.

That evening, Gordon was in his room pondering the problem when there was a ring at the door. It was Davinder. He'd come to explain that he couldn't play the cup match against the Polecats. It was his sister's wedding and there was no way his parents would allow him to play.

Gordon heard the news with relief but tried to look disappointed.

'Sorry,' Davinder said. 'I'll be there for the next round, though. You'd better win.'

''Course we will,' Gordon said.

He was on the phone to Oliver as soon as Davinder had gone. 'You're in the team against the Polecats,' he said. 'Davinder can't play.'

'Great,' Oliver said drily. 'I'm looking forward to that.'

On the Sunday before the cup match, the Wanderers' morale was boosted by a surprise three-two win against the Marvels who were third in the league. The Marvels scored first, Blondie crashing the ball in from a narrow angle. Then Gordon made two crucial point-blank saves and, rather against the run of play, Ahmet equalised after a Twink dribble and pass. In the second half, the Wanderers took the lead when Mark scored from a free kick only for the Marvels' striker to level the score with a close-range shot. The Wanderers defended well, Dave doing a good marking job on Blondie, and they snatched a last-minute win when Mark, anticipating a back pass from a Marvels' defender, beat the goalkeeper to the ball and side-footed it into the net.

'Fantabulous!' Stanley exclaimed.

The Wanderers were elated. It brought them level with the Polecats who'd been crushed six-two by St George's.

'That should discombobulate them,' Stanley said.

'I don't know about that,' Gordon said, 'but it's going to be a tough match.'

At the Saturday training session before the big match, the Wanderers practised one-touch passing movements. They knew their passing had to be quick and accurate to avoid the onrush of Polecats.

'If you keep possession, make them run after the ball, they'll start to lose their cool,' Stanley advised.

'Then what?' asked Oliver.

'You'll have a psychological advantage,' Stanley said knowingly.

The first thing Gordon did when he woke up on Sunday morning was look out of the window to check on the weather. A white frost stiffened the grass on the lawn. A watery sun filtered through a milky sky. It didn't look as if it was going to rain. Gordon breathed a sigh of relief. Heavy, muddy conditions would have given the bigger, stronger Polecats a big advantage. Dry hard ground favoured the more skilful Wanderers.

'I'm glad in a way that Davinder's not playing,' Gordon's mother said over breakfast. 'After what happened last time.'

'He would've played,' Gordon said. 'Only it's his sister's wedding.'

'I don't suppose he's too sorry about that,' his mother said. 'He was very upset last time. Let's hope there's no nastiness in this match. If there is abuse from their side, you just report it to the referee. Or to me. Do you hear me, Gordon?'

'Yes, Mum,' Gordon said.

'They've been warned,' his dad said. 'They won't want to be expelled from the league.'

'What, no punch-ups?' Billy asked innocently.

The referee called Gordon and Darren Walters to him before the match started and gave them both a warning.

'I don't want any repetition of what happened last time,' he said. 'I shall deal severely with any unfair play. And you tell your players,' he told Darren, 'that if there are any complaints of abuse from them, the team will be disqualified from the competition.'

He made them shake hands and Gordon could feel Darren tightening his grip, trying to impress him with his strength.

'You've got a new player,' Darren observed with a sneer.

'So what?' Gordon retorted. He didn't think he owed Darren any explanations.

The Wanderers kicked off. The ball went from Mark to Ahmet, back to Patrick, across to Oliver, forward to Stuart, back to Patrick again, out to Twink on the right wing, with the Polecats running around frustrated at not being able to get a touch of the ball. Twink started to jink his way down the right touch-line. Immediately, two defenders closed in on him. Obviously, the Polecats had decided that Twink was the danger man and had to be stopped. Twink, finding his way forward blocked, passed back to Patrick who pushed it forward to Mark. Unfortunately, before Mark could control it, Darren Walters was on him and had taken the ball away from him.

Taking the direct route was always the Polecats' favourite tactic. Bang the ball into the opponent's penalty area and hope for a mistake or a lucky break. That was the way they'd been trained to play. It wasn't beautiful to watch but it was often effective, particularly against weaker teams or teams that were easily intimidated. So, with his forwards charging towards the Wanderers' goal, Darren booted the ball high and hard into the goal area. Daniel headed it out but only as far as Colin Wright. He kicked it forward and shot after it. Clyde lunged for the ball but, unluckily for him, Colin reached it first and Clyde's outstretched leg connected with Colin's ankle. Colin went down writhing in agony and clutching his ankle. The whistle blew.

'Sorry,'Clyde said.

The burly figure of Darren's father, bucket in hand, lumbered on to the pitch. Colin was still writhing. The referee walked over to see how he was.

'I hardly touched him,' Clyde protested. 'And it wasn't deliberate.'

'But it *was* a foul,' the referee said. 'Free kick.'

Darren's father arrived, out of breath, red-faced and angry. He banged the bucket down and gave Clyde a hard shove which sent him flying.

'I know your sort,' he shouted at him. 'You should be banned from the game.'

There was a moment's stunned silence. Everyone froze. Even Darren looked shocked. Then the referee exploded: 'You can't come on the pitch and behave like that. What sort of example is that to set?'

'You should send him off,' Darren's father said.

By this time, feeling that he'd made his point, Colin had stopped writhing and was getting to his feet.

'I'm in charge of this game,' the referee said, 'not you. Now since your player seems to have made a remarkable recovery, I'll thank you to remove yourself from the pitch.' And as Darren's father walked away muttering to himself, he called after him, 'And if there's any more behaviour like that, I'll have you banned from the touch-line.'

Clyde picked himself up.

'Are you all right?' asked Dave.

'That man's a headcase,' Clyde said angrily.

'Calm down,' Gordon warned him.

Colin Wright took the free kick two yards outside the penalty area. The Wanderers lined up in front of goal. Finesse wasn't Colin's strong point. He simply ran up and kicked the ball as hard as he could. It went high and wide, a wasted free kick as Darren was quick to point out to him.

The whole episode had a strange effect on the Polecats. They lost their edge, their aggression. Even the yells from their coach were less in evidence. And when the Wanderers scored, there was no-one for Darren Walters to blame but himself. It came after some neat triangular passing between Patrick, Ahmet and Mark who slid the ball out to Twink. Again two defenders ran to close him down but he immediately switched play to the other side. Stuart, who was completely unmarked, received the ball on the left wing, took it all the way to the byline and crossed hard and low. It was a difficult ball to defend against and Darren, rushing back, only succeeded in charging it into his own goal.

There was what sounded like a yell of pain from Darren's father. A cheer went up from the Wanderers' supporters and a scream of delight from Billy.

'Stupid,' the Polecats' goalkeeper muttered, half to himself.

'What did you say?' Darren said, squaring up to him.

'Well, it wasn't my fault,' the goalkeeper said.

'Yes, it was,' Darren insisted. 'You were out of position.'

The Polecats went on the attack after that but they had no natural wingers like Stuart and Twink and the Wanderers' back four, keeping their formation well, dealt confidently with the attacks down the middle. Colin Wright had one shot on target which Gordon brilliantly tipped over the bar. Once, the ball ran loose in the penalty area and Gordon ran out to smother it before a Polecat forward could reach it. Otherwise, the Polecats had few chances to equalise.

'One more goal will destroy them,' Stanley said as they came off at half time. 'They're already losing confidence.'

'You think so?' Gordon wasn't convinced.

'Have I ever been wrong?' Stanley said.

Patrick grinned. 'What a big-head!' he said.

They were all in good humour, pleased with themselves. They felt that at last they had the measure of the Polecats and they weren't going to let them back into the match.

They were shaken out of their complacency within a minute of the restart. From the kick-off, the Polecats attacked. Oliver failed to clear the ball. Mike was charged aside. Daniel slipped as he was about to make a tackle. Colin was through, one-on-one with the goalkeeper. Gordon ran out to give Colin less of the goal to aim at. He guessed that Colin wouldn't try and take the ball round him or sidefoot it into the corner. He'd just blast it. He was right. Everything seemed to be happening in slow-motion. He saw the effort and determination on

Colin's face. He saw him, barely two yards away, prepare to smash the ball into the goal with his right foot. He swayed from side to side, hands raised in front of his face. There was nothing he could do but spread himself, stand firm and hope that the shot would hit him. It did. Hard, painfully hard, on the right knee from where it ballooned over the touch-line for a throw-in.

'Great save, Gordon!' screamed Billy.

There was loud applause from the touch-line. Darren's father clutched his head as if in agony. Colin had his face hidden in his hands.

'How could you miss that?' shouted Darren.

The sigh of relief from Gordon's team was almost audible. Conceding a goal then would have been a disaster.

Halfway through the second half, the Wanderers increased their lead. For once, Twink shook off both his markers. He deceived one with a body swerve, skipped past the impetuous tackle of the second and cut inside. Mark called for the ball but Twink went straight for goal. At the corner of the penalty area, seeing Darren charging towards him, he tried a shot. Darren just got a boot in front and deflected the ball for a corner.

Twink raised his right arm to indicate that he was going to take a near post corner. Patrick took up his position. For almost the first time, Twink's corner was perfectly placed. Patrick jumped and headed the ball backwards. It went over the goalkeeper's hands to the far post. Stuart, Mark and two defenders all jumped for it but it was Mark who got his head to it and nodded it in.

The Wanderers were jubilant. Mark was mobbed. Twink did a handstand. Billy was doing a dance with Stanley on the touch-line. Gordon clapped his gloved hands together. He didn't want his team to get too excited. There were still fifteen minutes to play.

Darren was fuming. He went up to the referee and shouted angrily: 'That was a foul.'

The referee turned away and pointed to the centre circle.

'Didn't you see? He used his elbows.'

'Are you arguing with me?' the referee said.

'You need glasses, you do,' Darren yelled.

The referee produced a yellow card from his pocket. 'Any more from you and you'll be off,' he said.

The Polecats were never in it after that. They were demoralised. All the Wanderers had to do was pass the ball around, keep possession, make their opponents run about like headless chickens. Darren looked as if he was about to blow a fuse. The rest of his team seemed to have given up.

When the whistle blew for the end of the match, Gordon, much to everyone's surprise, called for three cheers for Park Hill United. There was a half-hearted response. They all waited for Darren to do the same but he made a rude gesture and rushed off the pitch.

'We won,' Patrick said as if he could hardly believe it.

'I knew we would,' Gordon said, grinning happily.

'So did I,' said Stanley. 'Now for the quarter finals.'

6

February – 'Go out and enjoy yourselves'

The Wanderers completed the first half of their league programme with a match against St George's which they lost three-one. They weren't too disheartened. St George's were top of the league with Allcroft Albion and had some extremely skilful players. So only losing three-one wasn't, they thought, such a bad result. Anyway, all their hopes now were concentrated on the League Cup. In the next round, they'd been drawn to play against Watlington United (the Wattles for short), a team lying mid-table in the first division.

'Oh well,' Dave said. 'At least, we got to the quarter-finals.'

'And when we beat them, we'll be in the semi-finals,' Gordon said.

'Beat them!' Dave exclaimed. 'You're dreaming.'

'Well,' said Gordon. 'Why not?'

'They're in the first division.'

'I told you. Giantkillers. Little teams beating big teams. It's always happening in cup games.'

'It does happen,' Mr Roberts intervened. 'I remember Sunderland beating Leeds in the Cup Final when Sunderland were in the second division.'

'Told you,' Gordon said. 'We're going to win the cup.'

'If we did,' Dave said, 'I'd be' – he tried to think of a strong enough word – 'totally amazed,' he said at last.

'You'd better believe it,' Gordon said.

A week before the cup match was due to be played, Gordon's mother was notified that Park Hill United had withdrawn from the league and so had defaulted the rest of their matches.

Gordon asked a boy at school who was a friend of the Polecats' goalie what had happened.

'Half the team refused to play with Darren any more,' the boy said. 'They got sick of being shouted at and bullied by him and his father. The team just fell to pieces.'

'Good riddance!' Ahmet said when Gordon announced the news to the rest of the team.

'Yeah, I'm glad we don't have to play them again,' Patrick said.

Davinder said nothing but Gordon could see the relief on his face.

Four days before the cup match, the rains came. Every morning, Gordon woke up and ran to look out of the window and every morning his heart sank as he saw the sheets of rain flooding down from a murky sky. The pitches were waterlogged, the matches postponed. The cup match against Watlington was put back to the first week in

71

February. Rain and sleet fell almost non-stop for two weeks. Then, suddenly, the dark clouds blew away, the bright, cold weather took over and the football games resumed.

At the end of January, the Wanderers played the return match with Barnside. They drew three-all, which, considering they'd been beaten in the first match, was, they all felt, proof of their improvement.

Stanley missed that match. He'd been sent to watch the Wattles play a first division league match. The following Saturday, the whole team assembled in Gordon's house to hear his verdict.

'They're good,' Stanley said, 'but not that good. I don't think they're as good as St George's or the Albion.'

'But they're better than us,' Patrick said.

Stanley took his glasses off to clean them with a grey handkerchief.

'It's a cup match,' Gordon said impatiently. 'Anyone can beat anyone in a cup match.'

Stanley replaced his outsize spectacles and blinked. 'They've got a dangerous striker called Victor,' he said. 'They rely on him a lot. He's big and strong and fast and he's got a powerful shot.

If we can mark him out of the game, we've got a chance.'

'That's your job, Dave,' Gordon said.

Dave groaned.

'Patrick should follow him around as well,' Stanley said. 'Make sure he doesn't get any shooting chances.'

'Anything else?' asked Gordon.

'They'll probably expect to beat you,' Stanley said, 'so they may be over-confident. If you play like in the last few games, you could surprise them.'

'That's it,' Gordon said. 'Take them by surprise. Score before they realise how good we are.'

'Yes,' Patrick said. 'That should—' he looked at Stanley and grinned '—discombomble them.'

'Discombobulate,' Stanley corrected.

'I know you want to win,' Gordon's mum said, 'but what about enjoying yourselves? Isn't football supposed to be fun?'

'It's more fun when you win, though, Mrs Roberts,' Patrick said.

'Well, I'm going to enjoy myself,' Mike said. 'I don't care what happens.'

'Good for you, Mike,' Gordon's mum said. 'Go

out and enjoy yourselves. Isn't that what managers tell their teams before a big match?'

Stanley nodded knowingly. 'I believe so, Mrs Roberts,' he said. And then he added almost to himself: 'It must be fun to play football.'

Gordon's mum looked at Stanley's long sad face in surprise. 'I'm sure it's just as much fun playing chess,' she said.

Stanley's face lit up. 'I love playing chess,' he said. 'It's fantabulous. I love it more than anything. I forget everything when I'm playing chess. I can be the champion of the world when I'm playing chess.'

'There you are, then,' Mrs Roberts said.

'I still wish I could play football,' Stanley said. 'I dream about it sometimes. They wouldn't make fun of me if I played football.'

'Who makes fun of you?' demanded Mrs Roberts.

'We don't,' Gordon said. 'Not any more.'

'They wouldn't dare,' said Mrs Roberts. 'Where would they be without you?'

'That's right,' said Gordon. 'You're our secret weapon.'

'Don't tell him that,' Patrick said. 'His head's big enough as it is.'

'Take no notice,' Mrs Roberts said. 'You've got the footballing brain in this team. That's just as important as being able to kick a ball around.'

Stanley looked at her gratefully.

'Yeah,' Patrick said grinning. 'Where would we be without your footballing brain?'

'Remember that,' said Stanley.

For the first time, Gordon felt nervous before a match. He couldn't eat anything for breakfast and when they arrived at Watlington's home ground and he saw the crowds of supporters who'd turned out to watch, his stomach felt wobbly. Supposing he did something stupid and let in an easy goal? He shook his head. It wasn't going to happen. I'm a good goalkeeper, he told himself. But that didn't seem to cure the flutter in his stomach or the dryness in his mouth.

It was the best ground they'd ever played on. There were proper changing rooms with showers and a little wooden café alongside.

'Makes you feel important,' Patrick commented as he put on his football boots.

'One day, we're going to have our own ground like this one,' Gordon said.

'He's dreaming again,' Dave mocked.

Once they were on the pitch, kicking the ball about, Gordon felt a little better. Most of the crowd would be cheering for the Wattles but the Wanderers had their loyal followers too – mostly dads and brothers, plus a few mums and schoolfriends.

'Have you seen that striker Stanley was talking about?' Dave asked. 'Victor. I can't believe he's our age.'

Gordon looked across to the Watlington team where a tall, muscly boy was limbering up.

'He must eat boxes and boxes of cornflakes,' he said.

Davinder looked over to the touch-line. 'What's Darren doing here?' he asked.

'Where?' Gordon followed the direction of Davinder's gaze. He saw Darren standing on the touch-line with a boy who'd been with him at Greenfield Park after the football practice.

Gordon shrugged. 'You can't stop him watching the match if he wants to.'

'I hate it,' Davinder said. 'Feeling his eyes on me all the time.'

'Just ignore him,' was Gordon's advice.

It was a bright breezy day. Gordon won the toss

and decided to play the first half with the sun behind him. He still felt a bit nervous and didn't want to start off with even a weak February sun in his eyes. His greatest fear was that his team would be demolished ten-nil and everybody would laugh at them.

The Wattles kicked off and almost immediately forced a corner. It was an outswinger and when the ball came across, their striker, Victor, jumping higher than anyone, headed it firmly towards the goal. It thudded against the crossbar with Gordon nowhere. Daniel and Clyde between them scrambled it away.

Gordon was shaken. That was a let-off. And it would have been his fault if they'd scored. He hadn't even seen the ball let alone been in the right position to save it. He took deep breaths to calm himself down.

The ball was now bouncing around the midfield. Neither side seemed to have settled down, taken control of the game. There were too many misplaced passes. A half-hit pass from Patrick was intercepted. The ball went forward to Victor. His strength and speed took him past nervous tackles from Davinder and Dave. Miraculously, it was

Mike who stopped him with a well-timed sliding tackle. Clyde was on hand to poke the ball back to Gordon who whacked it into touch.

'Well tackled, Mike,' Gordon shouted, clapping his gloved hands together.

Mike beamed happily. He rarely did anything to deserve that sort of praise.

From the throw-in, the Wattles attacked again. It was then that a dog decided to join in the game. A brown-and-white foxhound pulled away from the stout woman who was his owner and, barking excitedly, bounded after the ball.

'Get that dog off!' shouted the referee.

The game stopped. A Watlington player picked up the ball. The dog stood stock still on the pitch and barked furiously, demanding to be allowed to play. Patrick and Davinder made a grab for him but he evaded their grasp and raced off. The stout woman wobbled on to the pitch.

'Winston!' she called. 'Come here! Come here at once!'

The dog ignored her. Soon the game of football had turned into a game of chase-the-dog. Everyone, including the stout woman and the referee, was running round in circles after the dog and

making spectacular dives to try and grab hold of him but the dog, excited by this new game, was too quick for them.

The spectators were applauding and laughing and shouting instructions. After five minutes of this, Gordon was laughing so much he had to sit down to recover. Eventually, the referee managed to grab hold of the dog's collar and hand him over to the stout woman.

'Keep that animal under control,' the referee said.

The woman apologised. 'I don't know what got into him,' she wheezed, trying to catch her breath. 'He's never done that before.'

'Well, make sure he doesn't do it again,' the referee said. 'This is a football match not a dog show.'

The incident seemed to affect the Watlington team's concentration. They lost their momentum, their sense of urgency. Gordon's team, on the other hand, relaxed. Gordon himself felt the nerves and tension fall away from him. He was ready to enjoy the game. It *was* only a game after all.

The game restarted with a drop-ball. Davinder won it and pushed it forward to Mark. A quick one-two with Ahmet took him round one defender and then he switched play out to Stuart on the left wing. He raced along the touch-line with the ball and then, as a defender came to tackle him, performed his favourite trick. He swung his left foot as if he was going to centre the ball but at the last moment turned it back between his own legs. Usually it didn't work. This time it did. The defender flung himself forward to block the centre, leaving Stuart free to take the ball towards the goal. As another defender came to tackle him, he turned the ball back to Mark who, from five yards out, drilled it into the back of the net.

A brilliant goal!

The Watlington team were stunned. They'd fallen behind after doing all the attacking. The second division side had scored first. What a nerve!

Gordon clapped his hands and shouted to his team to keep calm, not to do anything rash. They were under sustained pressure for the rest of the half but managed to hold out. Gordon performed heroically, saving a point-blank shot from Victor and turning a long-range effort round the post. The Wanderers might even have gone further ahead when Twink, after turning the left-back inside out, found himself with only the goalie to beat but stumbled as he was about to shoot, allowing the keeper to take the ball off him.

Still, the Wanderers came off at half-time with their confidence high. If they could only hold on to their lead – but could they?

'You're playing well,' Stanley said, 'but you're giving Victor too much room. He looks as if he's going to score every time he gets the ball.'

'We're doing our best,' grumbled Dave. 'You try marking him.'

Stanley hunched himself up into his overcoat. He didn't enjoy that sort of remark.

'He's still here,' Davinder muttered.

'Who?' asked Patrick.

'Darren Walters.'

'I thought I saw him,' Patrick said, glancing over to where Darren was standing glaring at them. 'Perhaps he's come to see how football should be played.'

'He keeps staring at me,' Davinder said. 'It's giving me the creeps.'

'Take no notice,' Gordon said.

'No,' said Davinder, 'I'm going to ask him what he's doing.'

'Davinder!'

'Leave him,' Mrs Roberts said, laying a hand on her son's arm. 'Just watch him in case there's any trouble.'

'I'll keep an eye on him,' Mr Roberts said. 'At least his awful father doesn't seem to be around.'

Davinder planted himself directly in front of Darren and looked straight at him. 'Enjoying the match?' he asked

'You'd better keep out of my way,' Darren growled threateningly.

'I thought it was you following *me* around,' Davinder said.

'It's a free country. I can go where I like.'

'So can I,' Davinder said.

'You shouldn't be here at all. You should go back where you came from.'

Davinder stared at him in amazement. 'I was *born* here,' he said. 'This *is* where I came from.'

'Liar!'

'Do you want to see my birth certificate?'

'You know what I mean,' Darren shouted aggressively.

'No, I don't.'

'And you told lies about me.'

'No, I didn't,' Davinder said, trying to keep control of himself, trying to keep calm. 'You swore at me. You called me names.'

'What if I did?'

'So I didn't tell lies about you.'

'You got us warned by the league,' Darren accused. 'And now my team's broken up.'

'That's not my fault,' Davinder said. 'It's not my fault if the rest of your team don't want to play with you any more.'

'Who told you that?'

'Everybody knows that, Darren.'

''Cause of my dad, not me,' Darren said bitterly. 'And now my dad's blaming me. He won't even talk to me any more.'

Davinder looked at him in surprise. Was this the Darren Walters everyone was afraid of? Was this the threatening figure who'd upset him so much on the football field? His father probably bullied him, Davinder thought. That's why he takes it out on everyone else. He even felt a pang of sympathy for him.

'Look,' Davinder said, trying to sound friendly, 'I'm sorry your team broke up, honest I am. But you can't say it was anything to do with me. So—' he held out his hand, not really expecting Darren to accept his gesture, not really knowing what to expect, '—if you want to shake hands, we can forget all that stuff.'

Darren stared at the outstretched hand. His fists clenched. For a moment, Davinder was sure Darren was going to punch him in the face but he didn't retreat, didn't withdraw his hand. The silent boy who'd listened impassively to the whole conversation laid a restraining hand on Darren's arm. There was a tense moment which seemed to Davinder to last for ages as he stood there with his hand outstretched. Then Darren looked at the ground and, with careful deliberation, spat. A gob of spit just missed Davinder's right boot. Darren turned and walked away, followed by his silent friend.

Davinder let out a long sigh of relief and ran back to join the rest of the team.

'What happened?' asked Gordon.

'Nothing,' said Davinder. 'We had a chat, that's all.'

'Has he gone?' asked Patrick.

'I think so,' Davinder said. 'I hope so.'

'Good riddance!' Ahmet said.

The whistle blew for the start of the second half.

'Don't forget,' Stanley called. 'Victor's the danger man.'

'Don't worry,' Patrick said. 'Me and Dave'll look after him. He won't get a touch of the ball in the second half.'

Unfortunately, Patrick's prediction proved over-optimistic. Even with two players marking him, Victor threatened danger every time the ball was passed to him. All the Wattles' attacks were focused on him. Five minutes after the restart, they equalised. A centre from the left wing was met by Victor on the volley and the ball zoomed into the net before Gordon could move. A relieved cheer burst from the Watlington supporters. A few minutes later, they had something more to cheer about. Again Victor was involved in the goal. He sent Patrick the wrong way, took the ball round Mike, made space for himself on the right and let fly. Gordon leapt to his right and got a hand to the ball but could only push it out to the left winger who headed it back into the net.

Disconsolately, Gordon picked the ball up and booted it upfield.

'Oh well,' Dave said. 'At least, we got to the quarter-finals.'

'We're not out of it yet,' Gordon told him. 'We can still win.'

'Dream on,' Dave said.

Gordon mused afterwards on how football matches could suddenly swing round and favour the team that had been losing. The dog running on the pitch had robbed Watlington of their momentum and given the Wanderers their chance to score. Now the second goal putting Watlington in the lead had the effect of making them complacent. They thought they'd done enough to win and could take it easy and play out time. This allowed Gordon's team to go on the attack, pressing the Wattles back. Gordon ordered Patrick and Davinder upfield. They had to take risks in the search for an equaliser. Watlington brought their players back to defend, leaving Victor a lonely figure in the Wanderers' half.

Gordon watched the action at the other end on tenterhooks. Would his team manage to score before the final whistle? How long was there? Surely the Wattles had too many defenders back. The way through seemed blocked. He saw Twink sell the Watlington left back a perfect dummy and, as another defender moved to challenge him, swing the ball into the crowded goal area. He saw Patrick, standing on the corner of the penalty box, jump for the ball and head it backwards. He saw it loop high over everyone, touch tantalisingly the keeper's outstretched fingers and lodge in the top corner of the net.

'Ye-e-s!' he screamed and did a jubilant dance in his goalmouth.

The Watlington players could hardly believe it. They thought the game was as good as won. Now they'd have to do it all over again.

'How long to go?' Ahmet asked the referee.

He looked at his watch. 'About three minutes,' he said.

'What happens if it's a draw?'

'Ten minutes each way extra time,' the referee said.

Ahmet groaned. 'I'm flaked out,' he said.

The referee smiled and blew his whistle for the restart. Now it was the Wattles' turn to throw everything into the attack. Victor charged forward trying to force his way through. Clyde tackled him. The ball ran loose. Mike half-cleared it. His legs felt like lead. The ball bounced from player to player. Davinder got a boot to it and kicked it high upfield. Anywhere would do. It bounced over the heads of two defenders. Mark raced for it, the two defenders snapping at his heels. The ball bounced towards the goal. Mark urged his tired limbs on. The goalkeeper hesitated and then decided to come out. Too late. Mark reached the ball a fraction of a second before the keeper and toe-poked it into the empty net.

Pandemonium on the pitch and on the touchline.

Mark collapsed, exhausted.

Crestfallen expressions on the Watlington faces.

The whistle blew for the end of the game. The Wanderers had won three-two. They'd beaten a first division side. They were in the semi-finals.

Despite their disappointment, the Watlington team and their supporters sportingly applauded the Wanderers off the pitch.

'What do you think of that?' an exultant Gordon asked Dave.

'Amazing,' Dave said. 'I'm – amazed. I'm totally amazed. I'm amazingly amazed.'

'Giantkillers,' Gordon said. 'Told you.'

7

March – Last minute rescue

The four teams left in the League Cup were West Side Wanderers, Allcroft Albion and two first division teams, Tottington Manor and Stoneleigh Villa. The Villa had knocked out St George's in the previous round. When the draw was made, it pitted the two first division sides against each other and Allcroft Albion against the Wanderers.

'I bet the Albion are pleased,' Gordon said. 'I bet George and his dad are jumping up and down with delight. I bet they think they'll beat us easily.'

'They already have,' Dave reminded him. 'Five-nil.'

'We've improved since then,' Gordon said. 'And anyway this is a cup match. I told you – anything can happen in a cup match.'

'I know,' Dave said. 'We did beat the Wattles. But they're not as good as the Albion. They're a one-man team. All Albion's players are good. They'll be in the first division next season.'

'It's up to us to find out their weaknesses,' Gordon said.

'They haven't got any.'

'They're not Liverpool. They're not Manchester United.'

'George's dad thinks they are,' Dave said.

''Course they've got weaknesses,' Gordon insisted.

'Aren't we playing them again in the league before the semi-finals?'

Gordon nodded. 'And that's when we'll find out their weaknesses.'

Allcroft Albion always attracted a big crowd to their matches. They were still unbeaten in the league and were now in the semi-final of the League Cup. According to Clyde, who was a friend of an Albion player, scouts from professional teams had been along to watch George. The Albion were everyone's favourite to be promoted to the first division.

Gordon was encouraged by the way his team played that day. They still lost four-two but were, he thought, a bit unlucky. Ahmet shot inches wide, Mark headed against the crossbar and Twink tried shooting when he should have passed to Mark who had the goal at his mercy. It could have been different, Gordon thought. But then, he had to admit, every match could have been different. What counted was not the match that could have been but the match that was.

As he walked off the pitch, he noticed one of the spectators, a tall, dark-haired girl, waving to him.

It was Denise, George's sister. It was ages since he'd seen her. He hadn't recognised her at first. She looked different – older for one thing, and a lot taller than when she was playing for the Wanderers as striker. She'd scored some good goals, Gordon remembered. It was a pity she'd given up football for basketball.

'Not a bad team you've got,' she said as he greeted her.

'Thanks. We got beat though. We're always losing to your brother's team.'

'My dad's a good coach,' Denise said, 'that's why.'

'You still playing basketball?'

'Yeah. It's a great game. Makes you grow tall.'

'Does it?'

Denise laughed. 'Can't you see?'

Gordon flushed and looked down at his boots.

'Just a joke,' she said.

'What about football?' he asked. 'Don't you miss it?'

'A bit. I dream about it sometimes. I'm always scoring the winning goal.' She laughed again.

'I have nightmares about football,' Gordon said. 'Everyone's pointing at me because I've let in ten goals in the cup final.'

She smiled. 'You made some good saves today though.'

'Thanks. We've got to play the Albion again in a couple of weeks.'

'I know,' she said. 'Semi-final of the cup. George thinks he's already in the final. He thinks they'll beat you easy.'

'Anything can happen in a cup match,' Gordon said.

'You going to win then?'

'I hope so.'

'So do I,' Denise said. 'My brother's head's getting so big it'll burst soon.'

'Are you going to come and watch?'

'I might,' she said.

Mr Harker, Denise's father, came striding towards them and shook Gordon's hand. 'Well played, lad,' he said. 'You've done well. Getting to the semi-finals an' all. Bit of a surprise that.'

'We raise our game for cup matches,' Gordon explained.

'Is that right?' Mr Harker grinned. 'I'll have to remember that.' He put his hand on Denise's shoulder and, giving Gordon a knowing wink said: 'Pretty girl, isn't she?'

'Dad,' protested Denise.

Gordon stared at his boots.

'See you at the cup match, lad,' Mr Harker said.

The Wanderers played two more league games before the semi-final. First they beat Kingswood five-two. The next week they played Forest Rangers (with a different coach who, to Gordon's relief, didn't continually bellow instructions from the touch-line) and won three-one. They were still only fifth in the league, one point behind Barnside but it was on the cup that all their hopes and dreams were now centred.

The team met at Gordon's house the day before the crucial match to discuss tactics. Gordon tried to argue that with a bit of luck they could have won the last match against the Albion.

'I'm sure we can beat them,' he said.

'How?' asked Patrick.

'George and Bernie make a really good partnership up front,' Davinder said. 'They're always going to score goals.'

'We've just got to score more than them,' Gordon said.

'How?' asked Patrick again.

'You said we'd find out their weaknesses in

the last game,' Dave said. 'Well, I didn't see any weaknesses.'

'Their defence isn't that good,' Gordon asserted. 'We scored two goals and we could've scored more.'

Twink shook his head. 'That left back was hard to beat,' he said. 'And when I did beat him there was always someone covering for him.'

'If I could make a suggestion,' Gordon's father intervened. 'I think you need to get more players into the attack. When Twink or Stuart were going forward, they couldn't find anyone to pass to because Mark and Ahmet were well marked.'

'I did lose my marker sometimes,' Mark pointed out, 'but Twink never passed the ball.'

'But if Patrick and Davinder joined in the attack, and maybe even Daniel and Dave, you'd outnumber them. What do you think, Stanley?'

'Good idea, Mr Roberts,' Stanley said. 'I've been thinking—'

Patrick groaned. Dave and Clyde cheered.

'I think,' Stanley went on, ignoring them, 'we should change our formation. Put more players in midfield. Play three-four-three.'

'What for?' Patrick asked.

Stanley raised his finger as if he was about to make an important announcement. 'Whoever controls the midfield controls the game,' he said.

'Who told you that?' Clyde demanded.

'It's obvious,' Stanley said. 'It's like controlling the middle of the board in chess. That's where the game's won and lost.'

'I don't see the point,' Dave argued. 'I don't see how it makes any difference what formation we play.'

'I think it's a good idea,' Gordon said. 'If we play—' he paused and thought for a second, '—Davinder, Patrick, Ahmet and Daniel in mid-field, then when Twink, Stuart and Mark are on the attack, they can move upfield in - support.'

'And what happens when we lose the ball?' Patrick objected. 'We won't have enough defenders.'

'You'll just have to run back and help the defence,' Gordon said.

'It's all right for you to say that,' Patrick complained. 'You don't have to run at all.'

'You don't have to jump and dive and risk getting your head kicked in,' Gordon pointed out.

'Well, I like the idea of going up into the attack,' Daniel said. 'I reckon I could score a few goals if I got the chance.'

So they took a vote on it and decided to play three-four-three. After all, what had they got to lose?

The semi-final was on a neutral ground at the Rossington Lane Football Club. It was even more impressive than Watlington's ground. The Albion had attracted a noisy crowd of supporters. The Wanderers felt excited by the atmosphere.

'Next stop Wembley,' Patrick said.

Gordon wasn't as nervous as he'd been in the Watlington match. It was only another game against the Albion, he told himself, even if it was a cup semi-final.

When they ran on to the pitch to the cheers of their supporters, they saw that the Albion were already practising shooting at one end of the pitch.

'They're wearing a brand new strip,' Dave said staring. 'Where do they get the money?'

'They've got a name on the back of their shirts,' Davinder said.

'Brian Jack Garages,' Clyde said. 'That's where they get the money. Sponsorship.'

'Well, I wouldn't wear a shirt with Brian Jack Garages on it,' Patrick said.

'Nor would I,' said Mike. 'My dad took his car there once and they charged him a fortune and ruined his engine.'

'When we win the cup,' Gordon said, 'they'll be queueing up to sponsor us.'

It was a dull March day. Heavy dark clouds lumbered across the sky. There was no sun and little wind. George won the toss and decided to kick off. Immediately, the Albion swept into the attack. The Wanderers' midfield were back helping the defence. Dave was right. It didn't seem to matter what formation they played, they were still penned inside their own half. Every time George got the ball, there was danger. He was fast, he was strong and his control was good. Dave and Clyde had been assigned to mark him but he still managed to get in some good crosses. One ball in particular was directed perfectly on to Bernie's head. Bernie was a powerful header of the ball. Fortunately, Gordon was in the right place to make the save. He held the ball for a moment and motioned to his defence to keep calm. Then he rolled it out to Dave who threaded a through ball to Patrick. Patrick took the ball forward and since no-one seemed inclined to tackle him went on over the half-way line.

'Close him down,' came a shout from George's father.

Immediately, two defenders closed in on him. Patrick sidefooted the ball to Davinder on his left who pushed it forward for Ahmet to run on to. He swung the ball out to the left wing. Stuart and an Albion defender raced for it. The defender would have reached it first but slipped, leaving Stuart free to take the ball to the byline and centre. Patrick, Daniel and Ahmet, instead of staying back, kept on running. The Albion defence was outnumbered. It was Daniel who got his head to the ball which fell nicely for Mark to strike it on the volley. The ball skimmed inches over the cross-bar.

'Ooh!' came from the spectators followed by spontaneous applause.

It was the first Wanderers' attack and they'd almost scored.

'Bad luck,' Gordon muttered to himself.

Still, it was the Albion who were dominating the game and looked the most likely to score. Gordon rescued his team time and time again, beating out shots from George and Bernie, cutting out dangerous centres, twice taking the ball off Bernie's head and once saving with his feet when Bernie was through. He felt elated, unbeatable. When once a shot did go past him, Dave was in the right place to head the ball off the line.

It couldn't last. The pressure was too great. The first goal came from George. He waltzed round

Dave, cut in from the right wing and, when Clyde came to tackle him, slipped the ball across to Bernie. Bernie's cleverly angled pass put George clear of the defenders and, when Gordon came out, he was beaten by a shot that hit the far post and rebounded into the goal.

Gordon wasn't going to waste any time feeling sorry for himself. He was determined they wouldn't score again.

'Come on!' he urged his team. 'Go for it!'

Five minutes later, the Albion did score again. A through ball found Bernie completely unmarked and, when Gordon came out to narrow the angle, he lobbed the ball over his head. Gordon turned to watch helplessly as it bounced gently into the net. He felt sick to his stomach.

'It's gonna be a massacre,' Bernie grinned at him.

'We'll see about that,' Gordon said between clenched teeth as he kicked the ball back to the centre circle.

The Wanderers had more of the game after that. The Albion seemed to relax, content to play pretty football to show how clever they were. Gordon could hear Mr Harker shouting angrily at his team to stop messing around but they couldn't regain their former dominance. They had a few long-range shots which Gordon dealt with easily. Then came a dangerous attack. George curled a centre across which Gordon couldn't reach. The Albion left-winger coming in at the far post had only to nod the ball down into the empty net. Instead, it hit the top of his head and ballooned over the bar. A loud groan arose from the Albion supporters. Gordon breathed a sigh of relief. That was a let-off. If they'd have scored then, the game would have been over. As it was—

'Perhaps our luck's in,' he said to Dave as he placed the ball for the goal-kick. 'Tell Patrick and Daniel and Ahmet to go into the attack.'

'They're sure to score again if we do that,' Dave warned.

'It's the same if we lose two-nil or ten-nil,' Gordon pointed out. 'We're still out of the cup. We might as well go all out to score.'

Just before half-time, the Wanderers pulled one back. It was Twink who made it. Although he hadn't been getting much change out of the Albion left back for most of the game, he was always willing to take him on. This time he tricked him. He took the ball towards the right touch-line and when the defender followed him, he suddenly changed direction, pushing the ball to his left with the outside of his left foot. Another defender came to tackle him but now the Wanderers had six players in the attack. Twink's pass found Mark who made space for a shot. The goalie could only push the ball out and Daniel, following up, banged the ball into the net. Daniel raised his arms in triumph as the rest of the team rushed to congratulate him.

'Great!' yelled Gordon.

The whistle blew for half-time.

'Well done!' Gordon's mum said as she handed her team bottles of water.

'Thanks, Mum,' Gordon said. 'At least we're still in with a chance.'

Patrick threw himself on to the grass. 'I'm shattered,' he said.

'You've got to go on the attack more,' Stanley said.

'We're doing our best,' Stuart complained.

'If you could score a quick goal,' Stanley said, 'they'd be discombobulated.'

'Simple,' said Gordon.

But it was the Albion who scored. George's

father had obviously said a few sharp words to them because they came out for the second half like demons. They forced three corners in a row. George took the third from the right wing and swung the ball across. Gordon tried to punch it out. Bernie jumped for it with both arms up. The next thing Gordon knew, the ball was in the back of the net. But Bernie hadn't headed it. He couldn't have done.

'That came off his arm,' Gordon protested.

Dave backed him up.

Bernie pointed to his head. The referee pointed to the centre spot.

Gordon was furious. That wasn't a fair goal, he was sure of it.

The Wanderers threw more players into the attack and made a few half-chances which they couldn't put away. But they left so many gaps at the back that the Albion had plenty of opportunities to put the game beyond doubt. Good luck and Gordon's goalkeeping kept the Wanderers in the game. George hit the post. Bernie scooped the ball over the bar when it would have been easier to score. And when they did get shots on target, Gordon seemed to have the knack of being in the right place. Again the conviction grew in him that he was unbeatable.

Five minutes to go. The Albion eased up. They'd done enough to win. They were content now to play out time.

Davinder intercepted a pass and took the ball forward. The Albion players backed off, waiting for him to pass the ball. Instead, he kept on running. A shout from George's father was followed by a lunging tackle which Davinder easily skipped round. His speed took him round another tackle and a quick one-two with Mark beat another defender. Suddenly, the Albion defence was breached. Four Wanderers attackers were converging on goal.

Davinder slipped the ball to Mark who side-footed it to Twink. As a defender rushed to tackle Twink, Mark screamed for the ball. For once, Twink did as he was told and Mark now only had the goalkeeper to beat. He made as if to hit the ball to the keeper's left and, when the goalie moved in that direction, directed it into the other side of the goal.

Amid the cheers and applause, Gordon heard his brother's voice screeching out: 'Great goal!'

The Wanderers wasted no time in congratulations. Mark picked the ball out of the net and
raced back to the centre circle with it. Perhaps
there was still time to score the equaliser. Gordon
was jumping up and down nervously in his goal.
One more goal, he told himself. They could do it.
They had to do it. Anything was possible.

'Keep possession!' yelled George's father as the
Albion kicked off. But, unnerved by the goal, they
were a little tentative now while Gordon's team
were fired up. Ahmet intercepted a predictable

pass to George and pushed the ball across to Patrick. The Wanderers streamed forward. The Albion rushed back. Patrick, deciding there was no time for a slow build-up, punted the ball hopefully forward. An Albion defender miskicked the ball to Twink. He flicked it over an outstretched boot, took two steps forward and crossed. The ball seemed to be floating harmlessly past the far post when Daniel, racing forward, launched himself at it. He connected with the top of his head, the ball hit the underside of the bar and went in. Three-three. The Wanderers had saved themselves at the last minute.

There was dismay on the faces of the Albion team and a stunned silence from their supporters. The Wanderers' fans cheered. Twink did a handstand in delight. Gordon could see Stanley and Billy jumping up and down on the touch-line. He himself felt strangely unmoved.

'I knew we could do it,' he muttered to himself.

But the game wasn't over yet.

Extra time followed. Ten minutes each way, play became scrappy. The players were tired. Neither team could make much headway. Even George was unable to make a breakthrough. At the end of extra time, the scores were still level. A replay had been ruled out because there was such a backlog of fixtures after the January rain. A penalty shoot-out would have to settle the game.

There was a five minute break while the teams recovered and decided on their penalty takers. Gordon selected Mark, Stuart, Patrick, Davinder and Daniel.

'Good luck!' they said to one another.

A toss of the coin gave the Wanderers the first penalty. The Albion keeper settled himself. Mark placed the ball, took a long run and thumped the ball. It scraped the bottom of the crossbar and went in. Mark raised an arm to acknowledge the cheers.

Bernie took the first one for the Albion. Gordon dived to his right. The ball went into the other corner. One each.

Stuart was next. He tried to sidefoot the ball into the corner but it was too soft and too obvious. The keeper saved it easily. Stuart hung his head and walked away. Davinder went to console him.

For the next one, Gordon tried diving to his left. The ball went over his diving body. If he hadn't moved, he might have saved it. Two-one to the Albion.

After Patrick had scored with his penalty kick, Gordon took up his position again. He could hear a hubbub of voices from the touch-line and even louder than that the sound of his own heart beating. He took deep breaths to calm himself. He told himself that he mustn't make a move till the ball was kicked. He crouched ready, his whole body tense, waited till the last second, saw which way the ball was flying and dived. He got a hand to it, pushed it on to the post and, as it rebounded to him, clutched it gratefully. He heard, as if from a great distance, the sound of cheers. They were back on level terms.

Davinder's penalty hit the post and came out. He put his head back and stared at the heavens as if asking what he'd done to deserve that. Gordon walked thoughtfully towards the goal. He had to save the next penalty to give his team any hope because George was taking the Albion's last penalty and *he* wasn't likely to miss. After his last save, Gordon felt strangely confident. The buzz from the spectators seemed to fade into the distance as the Albion penalty taker ran towards the ball. Again Gordon waited till the ball was kicked before deciding which way to move. In fact, he didn't have to move at all. The ball came straight at him. Still level pegging.

Daniel sent the goalkeeper the wrong way, scored in the corner and punched the air. Now it was up to George to save the Albion from going out of the cup. He placed the ball on the spot. Gordon watched him, sensing his nervousness. Even George, it seemed, could be shaky at moments like this. Gordon stood on tiptoe, alert, swaying from side to side, ready to spring. This was the crucial one. If only he could guess which side George was going to put the ball. He tried to shut everything out – the noise from the spectators, the anxious faces of Patrick, Dave and Davinder watching him, the Albion players shouting encouragement to George. He focused all his concentration on the ball as if willing it to go safely into his arms. The muscles in his legs felt tight. He hoped he wasn't going to collapse with cramp. George walked back ten yards. The crowd was hushed. The tension was unbearable. Some of the Albion team turned away, unable to look. George ran up quickly and swung his foot. Gordon jumped and saw the ball soar high over

the cross bar. It was unbelievable. He'd missed. George had missed. The best player on the field and he'd missed the crucial penalty. George buried his head in his hands and ran off the pitch. The Wanderers had won three-two on penalties. They were in the final.

8

April – The final game

Gordon couldn't remember much of what happened after the match. It all seemed like a dream. His team had beaten the Albion. They'd reached the final of the League Cup. Could it really have happened? He hardly heard the cheers and shouts of the spectators. He seemed to be floating in a world of his own. His elation was mixed with sadness for George. Not that George was a friend of his. But still . . . George would be feeling terrible missing that crucial penalty. Gordon hoped Mr Harker wasn't giving him a hard time. Anyone could miss penalties. Even the best professionals missed penalties sometimes. He'd seen it. He remembered wanting to tell George that. He vaguely remembered Mr Harker congratulating him and saying that the defeat would do the Albion good. It would give them a kick where it hurt. They were getting – what was the word? – complacent. And Denise. She'd been there, too. Said it had been a great game. Said he'd made some great saves. Said she hated penalty shoot-outs and hadn't been able to watch.

It took him a few days to come down to earth. He couldn't concentrate on anything at school. His mind kept going back to the match, to the penalty shoot-out, to the saves he'd made. When he wasn't remembering that, he was day-dreaming about the final. They'd be playing Stoneleigh Villa, one of the best first division teams, at Rossington Lane again. The Mayor would be there. And other important people. Just thinking about it made him nervous. He hoped the Wanderers wouldn't disgrace themselves, wouldn't get beaten out of sight. He didn't allow himself to dream that they might win.

The final was in April. Before that, the Wanderers completed their league programme with a draw against Mill Lane Marvels and a bad defeat, four-nil, against St George's. It could have been worse. They were never in the game. Their minds seemed to be elsewhere. So they ended the season fifth in the league. Not as good as Gordon had hoped. Next year, they'd do better. As expected, St George's and Allcroft Albion won promotion.

Now the cup final was all they could think about. No-one in the team seriously believed they could win it. But they were determined to play their best and to enjoy themselves. As Mrs Roberts told them, they might never get another chance to play in a cup final so they'd better make the most of it.

The day of the match dawned bright and sunny. Gordon woke up very early. It seemed to him that he hadn't slept all night, tossing and turning in a nightmare in which he kept picking the ball out of the back of the net. He ate his breakfast because his mother ordered him to but he felt sick afterwards.

The sickness persisted all the way to the ground and increased when he saw the crowds and the Mayor with a gold chain round his neck sitting behind a table with a silver cup displayed on it.

'You all right?' Dave asked him anxiously as they waited in the changing room to go out on to the pitch.

'I feel great,' Gordon said.

'I feel sick,' said Patrick. 'All my family are going to be watching. Hundreds of them. Brothers and sisters and cousins and uncles. One uncle's over here from Ireland.'

'My family aren't coming,' said Davinder. 'But I still feel shaky.'

'Same here,' said Ahmet.

'Have you seen the Villa team?' asked Stuart. 'They're bigger than us.'

'No, they're not,' Mrs Roberts said. 'They're young boys just like you. Stop worrying. You'll be fine. You'll give them a good game and you'll enjoy it. Or else!'

'That's right,' said Stanley. 'And don't forget all those things I told you about passing the ball around and making space for yourselves. Don't forget to move your rooks' pawns and your centre pawns up the board. Don't forget bishops move diagonally and rooks horizontally and knights jump over other pieces. And don't forget—' his voice rose to a shout '—the game's not over 'till it's checkmate.'

They all stared at him, baffled.

Patrick shook his head sadly. 'I knew it,' he said. 'His brain's gone. Poor boy.'

The sick feeling left Gordon as soon as the game started and he had to concentrate on defending his goal. The Villa in their blue and white striped shirts were a well-organised side with some skilful forwards and hard-tackling defenders. Their passing was good and, when they were on the attack, as they were for most of the first half, they never stopped running and looking for space. The Wanderers, playing three-four-three again, started nervously, miskicking and misplacing their passes as if they had no confidence in themselves. Gradually, though, they shook off their feelings of inferiority and managed to find more space to launch their own attacks. They had one good chance when Davinder, driving forward from the midfield, found Stuart unmarked on the left and his cross hit a defender and rebounded to

Mark. Mark's shot, though, went straight at the goalkeeper.

But it was the Villa who had the better chances. Again Gordon was called upon to perform heroics in goal. The Villa's two front players, Kevin Harper, their captain, and a boy they called Mo, combined brilliantly and caused the Wanderers' defence all sorts of problems. Desperate last-minute tackles from Clyde and Dave saved the day and then Gordon had to rush out and smother the ball when Mo was almost through. The goal, when it came, was beautifully worked. A pass from midfield found Kevin Harper who beat Mike and advanced on goal. Mo was to his left being marked by Dave. Clyde was running in from the other side. Kevin's pass forward bisected the two defenders and Mo, running round behind them, collected the ball, took it round Gordon as he raced out from his goal, and slotted it into the net. Gordon had to admit it was a deserved goal.

From the kick-off, the ball went out to Twink. He tried one of his mazy dribbles but a well-timed sliding tackle took the ball off him. Back came the Villa. A cross from the left found Kevin. He laid it off for Mo who struck the ball fiercely with his right foot. Gordon couldn't hold it but pushed it over the bar. When the corner came across, he rose above everyone and plucked the ball out of the air.

That was the last action of the first half. Somehow the Wanderers had kept the score down to one-nil but they'd have to do better than that in the second half if they didn't want to be trounced.

'You're playing well,' Stanley said as they sat in the changing room drinking orange juice. 'Only—'

'If you say anything about chess,' Patrick warned, 'I'll throttle you.'

'Chess?' Stanley looked at him innocently. 'You're confused, Patrick. This is football, not chess. I was going to say that you need to use the wings more. And you need to get more players forward when you're attacking.'

'That's what I think,' Gordon said. 'Let's go for it. If we could get one goal—'

'Stanley's right,' Twink agreed. 'I'm not getting enough of the ball.'

'You keep losing it,' Mark pointed out, 'when you do get it.'

'I'll beat that left back yet,' Twink vowed. 'Just wait.'

'Good luck for the second half,' Mrs Roberts said. 'And don't forget to enjoy yourselves.'

'We are,' Gordon said. 'Aren't we?'

'Ye-e-s!' came the raucous reply.

From the kick-off, Mark tapped the ball to Stuart who tapped it back to Patrick. Patrick made as if to take it to the left, then changed direction and switched it to Twink on the right instead. Twink turned and found the left back facing him. He showed the defender the ball, trying to tempt him into a lunging tackle, but the defender stood firm, watchful, waiting to see which way Twink would go. Suddenly Twink darted outside him and sprinted along the touch-line. The defender raced after him. Twink cut the ball back and the defender skidded past him. For once, Twink had the time to measure his cross. He saw Mark running towards the goal and tried to deliver the ball on to his head. But surely it was too far in front of him? Mark launched himself at it. The ball shot off his head and zoomed into the top corner of the net. The Wanderers had equalised.

Mark lay flat on the grass where he'd fallen

while he was mobbed. When he emerged, he was limping a little and grinning happily. That was the best goal he'd ever scored. He could see Gordon at the far end punching the air.

'Good goal,' Kevin Harper said as he prepared to kick off.

'Thanks,' Mark said.

The Villa pressed forward again, determined to regain the lead. All the Wanderers except Mark and Twink were back helping the defence. They had no time to pass the ball out. They were kicking it anywhere. Every time they got it clear, the Villa surged back again. There was a goalmouth scramble, the ball rebounded from Dave's legs, Kevin Harper stuck his foot out and there it was in the back of the net. Gordon had been completely unsighted. Two-one to the Villa.

The Villa pressed forward again. The Wanderers, showing great determination, managed some dangerous breakaway attacks but couldn't breach the Villa defence. Twink was being closely marked and whenever Mark got the ball, he would find two defenders snapping at his heels.

Towards the end of the second half, the pace of the game slowed. Davinder found himself with the ball in space. He moved forward with it and slipped it out to Stuart. He was immediately challenged and returned the ball to Davinder who'd kept running. Patrick also decided to move up into the attack. The ball came to Mark who was standing just outside the penalty area with his back to goal. Two defenders were in close attendance. There was no way through. Mark shielded the ball and then, seeing Patrick running towards him, released it at just the right moment. Patrick aimed a shot which the goalie moved to cover but it struck a defender on the leg and deflected into the other side of the goal. The Wanderers had equalised again.

A loud shout from the touch-line rose above the cheers: 'Good on you, Patrick!'

Patrick's freckly face turned red as he received the congratulations of his team-mates. 'That'll be my uncle,' he said.

Only ten minutes left. Could the Wanderers hold out and force extra time? Could they even snatch a last-minute winner as they had against the Wattles? Again the Villa pressed forward. The Wanderers' supporters watched tensely, willing their team to keep the ball out of goal. Then, as the

Wanderers launched another breakaway attack, it was the turn of the Villa supporters to have their hearts in their mouths.

There couldn't be much time left now. Ahmet and Stuart looked at the referee. Would he never blow the whistle? Their legs were aching. They didn't think they'd be able to run much more. They didn't want to think about extra time.

Patrick, tackling back, gave away a corner. Mo took it and raised both arms as a signal. It was an outswinger. Gordon couldn't reach it but Clyde headed it clear. A Villa midfielder headed it back. The ball came chest high to Kevin, standing with his back to goal. He tried an acrobatic bicycle kick. The ball went back over his head, over everyone's heads, over the outstretched arms of Gordon, under the crossbar and into the net.

The applause was thunderous. The Wanderers joined in. It was no shame to be beaten by a goal like that.

There was no time for the Wanderers to come back again. The final whistle went. Each side cheered the other. The Villa had won three-two, a deserved win. But the Wanderers hadn't been disgraced. They'd played well and given a good first

division side a close match.

Win or lose, they were going to have a party afterwards. But first they received their runners-up medals from the Mayor. Gordon showed his proudly to his mum and dad. His mum gave him a big hug.

'You were great,' she said.

'You'll play for England yet,' said his dad.

'Let me see! Let me see!' Billy demanded, jumping around excitedly. Gordon handed the medal to him.

'Wow!' Billy exclaimed. 'My brother's famous.'

'Not yet,' Gordon said. 'But I will be one day.'

They all met that afternoon at Gordon's. There were hot dogs and cakes and sandwiches and ice cream and fruit juice and spritzers. But before they started on the food, Gordon's mum made a little speech thanking them for the way they'd behaved during the season.

'You've been no trouble at all,' she said. 'And I want to thank Stanley especially. He didn't get a medal but he's been a first class manager.'

'And chess player,' added Patrick.

Stanley's white face turned pink but he looked as pleased as punch.

'You may not have won the cup,' Gordon's mum went on, 'but you've played some good football. And you've had a lot of fun. Haven't you?'

'Ye-e-s!' they all cried out.

'Fill the glasses, Gordon,' his mother ordered, 'and we'll drink a toast.' She raised her glass high. 'To West Side Wanderers,' she said.

'To West Side Wanderers,' they all replied. And broke into a loud cheer.

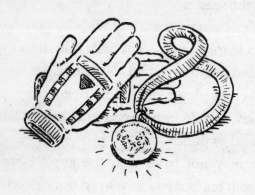